Margie Palatini

The Zoey Zone

SCHOLASTIC INC.
New York Toronto London Auckland
Sydney Mexico City New Delhi Hong Kong

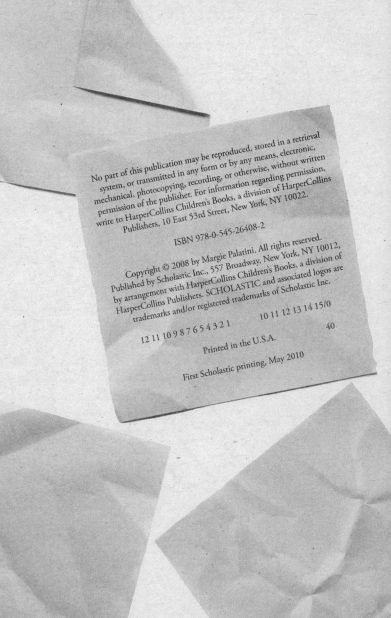

ISBN 978-0-545-26408-2

Copyright © 2008 by Margie Palatini. All rights reserved. Published by Scholastic Inc., 557 Broadway, New York, NY 10012, by arrangement with HarperCollins Children's Books, a division of HarperCollins Publishers. SCHOLASTIC and associated logos are trademarks and/or registered trademarks of Scholastic Inc.

12 11 10 9 8 7 6 5 4 3 2 1   10 11 12 13 14 15/0

40

Printed in the U.S.A.

First Scholastic printing, May 2010

My thanks to Venus, Alexis, Ashley, and Jaclyn for mucho inspiration; to Janine for her organizational skills; to Katherine for her support; and to my husband for his unending patience.

—M.P.

Since I'm eleven—well, almost eleven—
I'm thinking this really isn't
Chapter One of like my whole entire life.
(After all, I am almost eleven.)
This is probably more like
Chapter Forty-seven or
maybe even Fifty-one
(just so you know).
me: zoey zinevich

One
or whatever

So,

this is what I'm thinking • • •

Fairy Go

My b-friend, Venus, helped me with the lettering.

(She's also extremely excellent in cursive. Wait until you see page 8.)

Before you give yourself a total ha-ha snicker-fest, yes, I know, fairy godmothers are in that group with Santa Claus, the Easter Bunny, Tooth Fairy, Wish Upon a Star, etc., etc., etc. . . .

When you're eleven, you have entered the age of **SERIOUS DOUBLE DIGITS**, which means you are now:

(**a**) too old

or

(**b**) too cool to believe in that stuff anymore.

"You still believe in WHO?"

"WHAT?"

WARNING: followed by uncontrollable laughter by certain people who are (**a**) or (**b**) or both. Proceed at your own risk.

However, I'm thinking, me being an "almost" (as in technically ten) cancels out the (**a**) part (see above), and the (**b**) part (ditto on the above) is what I'm not—which is why I'm still allowed to think (**c**) fairy godmother.

4

This is a truly excellent thing, because I am not giving up Santa Claus—EVER—and being halfway to eleven is when you really absolutely need a fairy godmother the most. I'm going to require major fairy dust intervention in the hair department alone. There are just so many days a person can wear a hat, if you know what I mean.

Here's the spill (Venus-speak for "explanation"):

Sixth grade is only 198 days away. That's not a lot of time to learn about all the stuff you need to learn about. (And believe me, there's a lot of stuff to learn about that you NEVER even thought you needed to learn about.) Especially if you don't want to spend your whole life at

Table Ten.

Remember the hourglass and Dorothy? (Agree. You can never be too old for The Wizard of Oz.) Well, I'm down to those last grains myself. The clock is tick-tocking.

Venus says her sister says that if you're not cool

5

by sixth grade, you are not going to live happily ever after in sixth grade. The Cool Police are taking notes. *(Whoever they are, they're using a lot of paper on me already.)*

Being almost eleven is getting all very complicated. It's even way more complicated than one of Mrs. Helferich's word problems:

Person One walked from Town **A** to Town **C**.
It took **1** hour and **25** minutes to walk from Town **A** to Town **B**.
It took another **25** minutes to walk from Town **B** to Town **C**.
Person One arrived in Town **C** to meet **Person Two** at **2:45** p.m.
What time did he leave Town **A**?

I am definitely going to need outside help.

Especially in the previously mentioned hair and all-important accessorization categories.

I've fallen way behind in accessories.

It must have happened back in third grade when I wanted to be Amelia Earhart. The only accessory she had was a helmet. That was very useful for Amelia. Me too. The thing is, being almost eleven . . . you really can't wear a helmet to school anymore. Unless you ride a bicycle.

The backpack I made out of duct tape is pretty incredibly awesome, though. I'm just not sure The Bashleys (Brittany-with-two-Ts and Ashley, who are both accessory experts and "boing" on the coolability meter at Harry S. Truman) think a duct-tape backpack is a fashion accessory. Even if orange and purple is a truly outrageous color combination and duct tape is truly the most major astronaut accessory ever.

That's why I'm thinking about getting my own fairy godmother. Instant makeovers are FG specialities, and they know all about accessorization and "chic" too. (The Bashleys use that word all the time.)

According to my *Merriam-Webster Pocket Edition*, "chic" can be used as a noun or an adjective. Either way, it means "cool." So I've been researching fairy godmothers, and here's my Lightbulb Momento:

Cinderella

(Told you Venus is excellent in cursive.)

Do you know how many girls want to be a princess? Or act like a princess? Or look like a princess? Or want to find out that they *are*—but never knew they *were*—a long-lost princess?

One word: Google.

It's not just my little sister, Maddie, who is way pinked out at four and already wearing a tiara. I've found pictures of some pretty old people wearing those things on their heads.

I'm actually more of a green person, but I'm sure a fairy godmother can work with green. She can do chic in any color. More bippity and less boppity or . . . something like that.

Even with a good wand wave, I still might be a little tiara challenged. *(The hair situation.)*

Passing on those glass slippers too. I can't really fit in those tiny thingies anyway. My toes? Those shoes? These Chuck Taylor feet?

It's a long story about my big toe. Very ugly.
The toe and the story . . . maybe Chapter Ten. Remind me.

But, here's the really important what's what:

In the connect-the-dots world of frogs, princesses, and all kinds of fairies— you can include dragons, ogres, and wizards if you want because they are very popular too . . . especially in movies—a fairy godmother is only one dot away from Cinderella Dot Dot Dot, aha! who actually became a princess, which is very la-di-da, which means chic, which = cool.

The point being, as Mrs. Helferich likes to say when she talks about connecting dots, if it's okay to want to be a princess (and like I said, I've seen some scary pictures of old princesses), then it has to be okay to believe in a fairy godmother.

Especially if you're only almost eleven.

So . . .

I'm Going for it

(even if, technically, I am in double digits).

Presenting

"The Zoey Zone"

in

ZINE^VI_{SI}oN

A Zoey Zinevich In Your Dreams Production

VERY 21st CENTURY

Cue the Music!
(FYI—it's usually a harp.)

A teeny white light
suddenly appears!
Right in Mrs. Helferich's class.

Music gets louder
(adding a trumpet).

(Excellent special effects, right?)

The light is BLINDING!

What does it all mean?

"HUH?"
(The boys are clueless.)

Even The Bashleys have no idea
what's going on. "Huh???" x 2!

I am still an
almost-eleven believer!
I know! It is of course
an incredible . . .

FAIRY GODMOTHER MORPH!

Close-Up

She sees me. "Uh-oh. You need some fairy dust and fast!"

(Told you.)

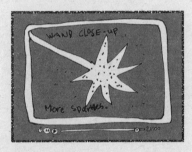

Zooming in on sparkles.

"Some bippity here. A little boppity there and . . ."

"WAIT!" (Close-up of Venus.)

"Don't forget her feet!"

15

"Even I can't do anything about her feet."

"Anywho, let's get to it! This girl needs a switcheroo by sixth grade!"

(I feel tingles. Not down to my toes, but close.)
AND THEN

16

Whoa!

"Who knew she could be
so la-di-da?"
"And chic! Definitely chic!"

"Used as an adjective
AND a noun!
With accessories!"

"Very you-know-what."

(I think it can work.)

Two

Samuel Morse-ing

• • • — — — • • •

(Just in case my FG is more 19th century.)

How to describe the Lunchroom at
Harry S. Truman School • • •

First, it is also the All-Purpose Room.

What that means is, when you're there and *not* eating, it still smells like what you *were* eating. Or worse, it smells like what you were doing.

It's the Gym too.

(I know. Who came up with that idea?)

Imagine how it smells in a place when you're stuck smelling the memory of everything and everybody that's ever been in that place.

It can all be *very* challenging nose- and stomach-wise. *Merriam-Webster* (pocket or regular edition) doesn't have enough adjectives to describe the aromas. I've checked. Pictures would definitely not be allowed either.

Especially of Alex Shemtob.

WAIT. *(Too harsh.)*

Alex is . . . okay. Sort of. Maybe.

I guess I do kind of like him. A little.

WAIT! *Backspace myself.*

ONLY in the *M-W* dictionary definition.
(Not, you know, in the other way. Please, I'm still officially only ten.)

However . . . Alex *does* know his history. He knows *almost*—and again I say *almost*—as much about the presidents as I do.

> Did I say "almost"? Because I want to make it known
> that I might be a presidential historian someday like that
> lady from Massachusetts who writes all the books my dad
> has on his bookshelves, and right now there's no contest that
> I know more about George to George and beyond than Alex
> Shemtob.
>
>   (Just want to clear that up.)

So, as history goes, Alex is in column A. He's quite the excellent one at solving word problems too. He's like the best mathlete at Harry S. next to Venus, who really knows her Sudoku.

And one more thing: He has primo pencils. He uses HBs, which are the best for filling in circles on multiple-choice tests.

But, good pencils aside, Alex needs a little SOS *(Samuel Morse and the scouring pads)* in . . . eating.

Venus describes it as "inhaling."

The thing is, Alex mostly exhales what he inhales.

Not pretty—or safe—especially if you're sitting across from him and not wearing an art smock.

But that's not the worst part that happens on this particular day 186 days before sixth grade.

Oh, not so hardly 🖤   🖤   🖤

Bring a box of tissues—or some of that pink stuff for your stomach.

You're going to need it.

The Lunchroom Life
of
Zoey Zinevich

Featuring Venus Romero
as her best friend

ACT 1: Scene 1

11:38 a.m.

Hot-Lunch Lunch Line

Venus and Zoey are last in the Hot-Lunch Lunch Line because they have stayed after library class to help Mrs. Temlock-Fields in the Media Center. Besides knowing Dewey and decimal, Mrs. T-F also knows Italian, which she is teaching to V and Z.

Today they learn *"bene,"* which means "good."

But . . . nothing is *bene* today.

Most of all lunch.

All the turkey sandwiches with or without mayo (no tomato) are gone.

V and Z grab their trays and slide along to the FIRST STOP on the Hot-Lunch Lunch Line: Mrs. Salerno, the hairnet lady with a mustache *(yes, mustache).*

She stares. Then grumbles.

(She is a very good grumbler.)

MRS. SALERNO:

Meat loaf or slumgullion*?

(*no known definition or description available at this time)

ZOEY:

Meat loaf.

MRS. SALERNO:

Gravy?

Zoey nods.

The spoon known simply as Super Salerno disappears into the murky *good word choice* goop. It comes back up (reemerges). *ditto on w.c.*

The gravy is thick, lumpy, and gray, which is a good thing. It covers the meat loaf, which is grayer.

Venus chooses the slumgullion.

(She really lives on the edge.)

Venus takes an apple.

Zoey takes an orange. *a healthy fruit, and her favorite color*

The two give their names to Mrs. Petrovic, who is the official **LUNCH LIST NAME CHECKER.** *Mrs. Petrovic checks the lunch list so nobody steals food. I know. Who would possibly want to steal gray meat loaf and slumgullion (whatever that is)?*

ACT 1: Scene 2
11:42 a.m.

V and Z are checked in and out.

They exit the Hot-Lunch Lunch Line.

And then . . .

realize the **HORROR OF IT ALL!**

The ONLY seats left in the whole entire Lunchroom slash All-Purpose Room slash Gym are at the tables of Alex Shemtob or . . . **The Bashleys!**

31

ACT 2: Scene 1
11:44 a.m.
Lunchroom/All-Purpose Room/Gym

Venus and Zoey stare down at their trays.

Mystery gravy?

Slumgullion?

. . . Alex Shemtob?

Their stomachs can't survive a Harry S. Hot Lunch and Alex.

V and Z have no choice.

They park their fannies at . . .

The Table Bashley.

A hush falls over the Lunchroom.

Even Alex Shemtob stops inhaling.

And exhaling. *Nobody* sits down at **The Table Bashley** *with* **The Bashleys** except *Friends* of **The Bashleys.**

Venus and Zoey are not *Friends* of **The Bashleys.**

They are not even *Friends* of the *Friends* of **The Bashleys.**

But—make no mistake about it—everyone wants to be a *Friend* of **The Bashleys** (see Chapter One).

Everyone at **The Table Bashley** stares. Then WHISPERS.

Whispering is NOT good.

NOT GOOD in capital letters when the WHISPERING is between

The Bashleys of **The Table Bashley.**

Venus and Zoey don't know what to do:

(a) Stare back

(b) Whisper between themselves

(c) Eat

It is not an easy multiple-choice.

The meat loaf and slumgullion are getting cold, which is—absolutely NOT GOOD.

And then . . . GASP!

THE BASHLEYS SPEAK!

Which is very incredible because they never speak to V or Z.
Ever. Well, maybe to say, "Move. You're in my way."

ACT 3: Scene 1
The Table Bashley

ASHLEY:
So . . . is it true that you both
are doing a "secret" science
report?

BRITTANY:
Sounds very "secret" . . . but,
you can tell us, right, Ashley?
We have no secrets at our table.

total spill   ZOEY AND VENUS:
It's on bullfrogs!

ASHLEY TO BRITTANY:

Fascinating!

Ashley and Brittany look at each other. They smile (Note: a very sneaky smile, so sneaky that V & Z don't even recognize it's sneaky, which is pretty sneaky).

Venus and Zoey smile back.

Backstory: They have been catching bullfrogs from the pond in Venus's backyard since they were four (supervised, of course, and wearing life jackets). They have caught, captured, and released three salamanders, a gazillion snails, dragonfly larvae (which are a little icky), two sunfish, six tadpoles, and seventeen frogs. Except for one frog the girls named Harrison, who is now Venus's pet because he is a champion slimer.

(His slime is more like spit than snot.)

They are working on a detailed, VERY secret journal with drawings.

Could it be that The Bashleys think Zoey and Venus are on the . . .

➤➤ **CUSP OF COOLNESS?**

primo word choice

ZOEY:

(very excited)

Bullfrogs are awesome amphibians!

Trust me. They totally are.

VENUS:

Want to come over to my house and catch one with Zoey and me? They're hibernating in the mud right now, but we can let you know when things start hopping.

(excited **and** punny)

The Bashleys look as if they have just swallowed Hot-Lunch mystery meat and a side order of slumgullion while

sitting across from Alex Shemtob
(and it's not because they didn't get the joke).

ASHLEY:

Frog catching? In the mud?

Eeeuuuuwwww!

BRITTANY:

Frog Crush! Frog Crushers!

Double eeeeeuuuww!

Sudden reality check for V and Z.
Catching bullfrogs is probably not in
any way totally or even semitotally
cool or awesome to Ashley and slash
or Brittany.

But—it is too late!

Venus and Zoey sink below plankton
on The Bashley HST food chain.

The Bashleys,
Friends **of The Bashleys,**
Not the *Friends* **of The Bashleys:**
Eeeeeeeeuuuuuuuwwwwww!

ACT 3: Scene 2
11:48 p.m.

Venus and Zoey are banished to

Table Ten.

As V and Z make their way down the
aisle of the Lunchroom slash All-
Purpose Room slash Gym with trays of
slumgullion and gray meat loaf, they
hear the not-so-soft WHISPERS from
The Table Bashley.

ASHLEY:
They will so never be cool.

BRITTANY:

Ever.

ASHLEY:

The only thing that will ever help them is a 9-1-1 massive cool transfusion.

BRITTANY:

Massive.

Venus and Zoey sit down across from Alex Shemtob at Table Ten and do their best to keep down the now cold and gray meat loaf and slum-gullion as Alex exhales.

It isn't pretty. . . .

They are not wearing art smocks.

The End.

Just so you know—if anyone wants to know—getting slimed by a frog
is unequivocally (mucho dollar word) incredible—
even if The Bashleys don't think it is.

(More on slime later if I have time.) z.z.

Three

Wait a secondo. This is only Chapter Three?
(Agree. That number two was a long one.
If you want, you can make this four.)

Or five.
Whatever.

Mom: Zoey? What are you doing?

Zoey Zinevich,

Come on Down!

It's time to Play . . .

"10 seconds before your Mother asks U a gazillion Questions!"

Is the correct answer:

(a)
I'm in my room doing nothing.

(b)
I'm in my room thinking about doing nothing.

(c)
I'm in my room thinking about a fairy godmother.

Me: Uh . . . nothing?

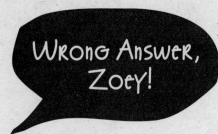

Mom: *Nothing?*

Me: (Uh-oh.)

Mom: How about cleaning your room?

I knew I should have gone with **(b)**.
I was thinking for one second to go with **(d)**
if there was a **(d)**—which would have been:

"I'm in my room working on my extra-credit history report about William Howard Taft."

Who, incidentally, was president from 1909 to 1913, which was slash is a whole other century ago.

(Googled him too. He is not even close to being as popular as any princess, real or pretend, which is sort of sad. After all, he was a president of the United States, and he was at the dedication of the New York Public Library—the one with the cool lions—which is a pretty big deal.)

In actual poundage, WHT was 332 lbs, which is how he got stuck in his bathtub. No, not even making that up! One most serious wedgie. Can your brain even digital a naked president of the United States having to get dewedged from a bathtub? In the White House! I will probably get extra extra extra credit for this.

(Venus and I have discussed. EEEC is not nerdy.)

So, absolutely, **(d)** would have saved me from cleaning up my room for sure, except my mom knows the report isn't due for two weeks, and even I wouldn't be working on it that far in advance. On a Saturday Morning?

When I usually stay in bed and peruse (a two-dollar word choice) my Scrabble dictionary?

Twelve days—maybe. But two weeks?

REALLY, that is just way too I'm-holding-my-stomach-from-laughing-so-hard unbelievable.

Only Simon Malachek and maybe Alex Shemtob, who The Bashleys think are both totally un-you-know-what, do stuff like that—and they are much more-more-more than I am. Much.

(Maybe delete-cross-out-erase the ditto "Much.")

Venus and I are still below fish food, chum bait, and frog scum in The World of Bashley Coolability. I stopped wearing green so they wouldn't *ribbit* every time they see me. Whenever my fairy godmother gets here, I'm thinking she is going to have to immediately bippity me over to the pink side. Which, truthfully, I'm sort of worrying about because . . . pink is not my color. Especially when it's pants. Then I look like a skinny stick of bubble gum.

Question:

Can a person be considered in any way cool if they look like gum?

Mom: Zoey? Are you straightening up your room?

Me: *Yeesh.*

Who can think about neatness when you're concentrating on extremely important stuff like finding a fairy godmother, William Howard Taft, or where-the-what you put your favorite shirt that has been mysteriously missing for almost three weeks and you can't find AnYWHeRE?

Stuff piles up when you are in deep thought.

I'm more naturally a piler slash multiheaper slash dumper than a folder-hanger-upper.

Hangers are way overrated anyway.

And btw, totally NOT environmental.

Interesting Factoid:
A person collects almost one thousand
wire hangers in his or her life, which
is enough to reach the top of
the Empire State Building
two times.

I'm just trying to do my part and live a green life. I keep telling Mom, "Piling may not be neat, but it is the absolute PC-EC way to go."

That, and using sticky notes.

Do you know how many trees I'm saving by using little pieces of paper instead of entire sheets? Practically an entire forest. Truly.

I wonder if I should do my entire President Taft report just on stickies?

Mom: Zoey?
Me: (Double yeesh.)

The Official Zoey Zinevich Guide to Cleaning Up Your Room

Step 1: Pick up. Pick up. Pick up.
Step 2: Open any drawer.
Step 3: Shove. Shove. Shove.
(Trust me. It really works. Try it.)

Actually, all this cleaning—well, sort of *cleaning* (I'm only almost eleven. I don't do bathroom swishing. Please!)—has me feeling very Cinderella-ish. Which I'm thinking might be very good, because so far I haven't hit the right century trying to contact my FG.

The only logical explanation I can think of is that there must be a whole lot of other people looking for a fairy godmother too. Since last Tuesday I've wished on twenty-seven stars, and still . . .

nothinG.

I'm going to have to come up with some other ways of contacting her, because those grains of sand are zipping along. There are only 184 days before sixth grade, when you have to be you-know-what.

If only she could just send me a sign. You know, point me in the right direction.

Hold the toilet brush!

Lightbulb Momento! (or maybe #2, 3, and 4 combined.)

What is peeking out from under PILE #3?

. . . Sock, jeans, sock, sock, hoodie, tank, Millard (my stuffed rabbit. What? You don't have a stuffed something? . . . Yes, you do), sock, PBJ sandwich (jelly still looks okay), sock, sock, striped tights, not-striped tights, plaid pants, sock, checked pants, seven dust bunny clumps (which make very interesting sculptures), sock, one dried-up paintbrush, flannels, notebook divider, a penny, blue sock, green sock, argyle sock, tee, overalls, violin case (I did Suzuki; now I play the piccolo), stale rice cake (not really sure how you tell if it's stale or not), broken tennis racket, underwear, more underwear (clean), two jigsaw puzzle pieces, Clue card (Mr. Green), four nickels, one dime, two tissues, soccer socks (eeuw, not clean), DayGlo marker, one crumpled crossword puzzle, five wicked chartreuse stickies, seven yellow LEGOs, sweatpants, retainer (so that's where that went), sock, sock (totally too many socks that don't even match), a roll of orange duct tape, and— Ta da!

My bowling shirt!

The Shirt.
In the Bedroom.
Under the Clothes.

Well, it's not exactly *my* bowling shirt, since I don't really bowl. (Except for that one time at Eugenia Vandopoulos's birthday party when I got nine gutter balls in a row. It was a record. For Eugenia's party and the bowling alley.)

This shirt belonged to my great grandpop. Aunt Rootie calls it "retro and very vintage." (I think that's good. At least it sounded good the way Aunt Rootie said it.)

Translated, I'm pretty positive it must mean "chic." I mean, what else could it possibly mean?

The shirt is turquoise with yellow trim *and* with monograms front *and* back.

Yes, well, of course my name isn't *Ray,* and I don't know who, what, or where is *Grabowski's Tool & Die Company.*

53

But . . .

I think it works.

Sort of.

Kind of.

Maybe.

Don't know.

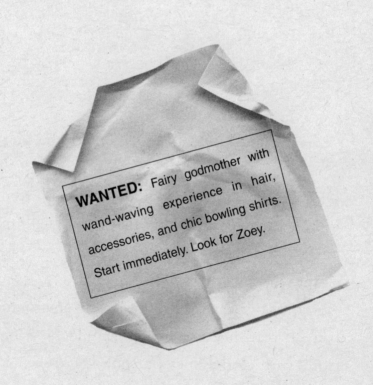

WANTED: Fairy godmother with wand-waving experience in hair, accessories, and chic bowling shirts. Start immediately. Look for Zoey.

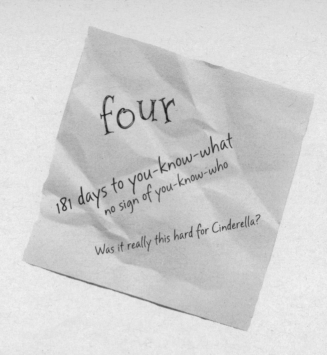

four

181 days to you-know-what
no sign of you-know-who

Was it really this hard for Cinderella?

Z.Z. Interesting Info Bite:

Did you know the first clothes dryer was invented in France in 1799? I think that is really stunning information, because who knew they even washed clothes in France in 1799?

Clothes dryers, while not exactly environmentally correct, because people should be hanging clothes on clotheslines but nobody knows what those are anymore, are still quite truly fabulous.

Especially when it comes to wrinkles.

And in spite of what happened to Fluffy. She was our kindergarten pet hamster, who one day ended up way too fluffed and very dead.

Billy Sherman took her home one weekend, and somehow she ended up in the Shermans' clothes dryer. It was all *molto tragico*, or *tristissimo* as Mrs. Temlock-Fields would say. Very sad. Venus and I cried for two weeks.

(Yes. That story might have to be a whole other chapter.)

Anyway,

it is because a clothes dryer is exactly such an incredible invention that hanging up clothes is so not necessary. Just a few spins on wrinkle-free and who needs hangers?

I keep telling Mom, "Heaping is good."

(A clothesline is way more EC, but it's a toss-up with using nine hundred hangers. btw: The bowling shirt looks *molto* excellent with no wrinkles, and definitely chic.)

The coolability meter is going to be rocked.

I think.

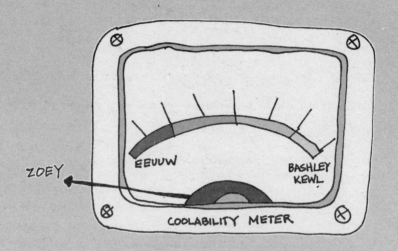

Uh-oh.

Here's a story
of a girl named Zoey
who was having
one bad-hair day
of her own . . .

Forgot the hair factor.

It's official.

My hair has been canceled.

Not even a fancy-schmancy barrette could save me. If I had a fancy-schmancy barrette.

If I was up to speed on accessorization, I might have a scrunchie. Or a headband. Or yarn. (Wait. Even I can't believe I just said yarn. My brain cells have been fried from that hair dryer—which, believe me, does not work as well as a clothes dryer when you're trying to get wrinkles out of your hair.)

Of course, I can't find any of my hats because—that's correct—I had to CLEAN my room!

I should have inventoried.
Or made a map.
Or sticky-noted.
Or made a map out of sticky notes.
Where is my

bucket hat?

(No. It's not stuffed in my dresser drawers.)

But what *is* stuffed in the third drawer, right-hand side, is my great-grandpop's fedora!

(which is one excellent name for headwear)

My great-grandma told me it's *spiffy*—which *Merriam-W* says is a word for "cool," which means "chic."

So—I think it might just WORK!

Or

maybe not.

BAD NEWS:

It only covers the top part of my head.

GOOD NEWS: It does go superbly with the bowling shirt. Especially the hatband with the yellow feather.

And (the best reason) it's the only hat I can find.

It may be even spiffy enough to stop anybody from connecting the dots to my • •

Hair!

"What's that weird thing on your head?"

Except for Maddie.

Stay tuned for an episode of
"Breakfast with Zoey"

Cornflakes

Bananas

1 Percent Milk *(I'm a little lactose intolerant.)*

a Cold Egg Roll

and a four-year-old sister.

"Zoey? Zoey? Zoey? . . . Zoey?"

"Yes . . . Maddie?"

"What's that weird thing on your head?"

"It's not weird."

"It looks weird."

"It's not weird."

"Looks weird."

"It's not weird. It's a hat."

"It's a weird hat."

"It is not a weird hat."

"Looks like a weird hat."

"It is not a weird hat. It's called a fedora."

"It's a weird hat with a weird name."

"It is not a weird hat, and it's not a weird name."

"It's an ugly hat with a weird name."

"You are only four years old, Maddie. You do not know what is weird or ugly."

"Yes I do."

"No you don't."

"Do."

"Don't."

"Do."

"Don't."

"Do."

"Don't."

"Do."

"Don't."

"MOM!"

"Girls. Eat your breakfast."

"Do."

"Maddie, stop squishing the banana in your fingers."

"Don't."

"Zoey, finish your cereal or you'll be late for school."

"Do."

"Maddie, stop picking your nose."

"Don't."

"Zoey, you don't really need to wear that hat. Your hair looks fine."

Doesn't.

"And please wear your heavy coat today."

uh-oh

". . . The poofy coat?"

"Zoey? You know what? That's even weirder than the hat."

Note to fairy godmother: Are you watching any of this?

Almost-eleven-year-old now spotted outside elementary school looking

like a poofy pumpkin. No fairy godmother in sight. Story at six . . .

Is this really only five?

five

Harry S. Truman Rule #5
ABSOLUTELY NO HATS ALLOWED.

It's THE LAW.

(Pretty sure this includes fedoras.)

Technically. . . . girls are allowed to wear hats at Harry S. because it's considered fashion and not plain old headwear. And while a fedora is incredibly fashionable, no disputing that,

> technically it was my great-grandpop's
> who technically was a boy,
> which technically might mean I am
> technically not allowed to wear it,
> technically speakinG.

Especially if Mrs. Pappazian sees me, because if there is one thing our principal is,

> it's technical.

Something tells me this isn't going to

> technically meet with her approval either.

Which means technically this could be an even worse day than I thought it would be since I am more than technically having a bad-hair day and looking like a huge, poofy pumpkin.

All of that, and because Mrs. Pappazian and I had a . . . sort of *debate* last Tuesday.

Spilling: You are never ever allowed to wear a hat during Assembly. (Assembly is when the All-Purpose Room is not being the Gym or the Lunchroom.)

But when the All-Purpose Room is being used for a gym and not an assembly, then it's okay to wear a baseball cap. However, it's also never okay to wear a baseball cap in the All-Purpose Room when it is the Lunchroom.

(Mrs. Helferich must have written Rule #5.)

So, last Tuesday during Assembly, Mrs. Pappazian, who has extremely excellent eagle eyes, immediately zeroed in like a dart on a bull's-eye to Walter—who was wearing a baseball cap. Walter not only loves baseball like I do (we had a long discussion one day when Venus and I were sitting at Table Ten), but he also has porcupiney hair.

From personal experience, I could tell that it was one of those very bad you-know-what days for Walter. He had to do something.

Yes! Even if rules were broken!

Therefore, dot-dot-dot, Baseball Cap.

It was all very logical.

And besides, we were in the All-Purpose Room slash Lunchroom slash Gym. Walter could have easily gotten all those slashes mixed up.

But Mrs. Pappazian didn't want to hear any logical explanations. She made Walter take off his hat in front of the whole entire school. And then kids started to laugh because his hair was sticking out all over the place. His face got all pink and splotchy, and his neck and arms started to polka-dot. Walter was changing colors right before our eyes! Nobody should have to get all pink and polka-dotted over bad hair.

Somebody had to say something.

So I did!

I stood up in Assembly and shouted,

"I Object!"

(That's lawyer talk from my favorite TV show that used to be on past my 9:30 bedtime but now is on almost every channel all day long. You can't miss it.)

I told Mrs. Pappazian that Harry S. Truman School should have an "open hat" policy for everyone.

"Fair and equal!
Bedhead equality!
Justice for all!"

(I think President Truman would have wanted that
from a school named after him.)

DUN DUND

(sound effect)

Mrs. Pappazian didn't agree.

Not about Walter.

The hat.

Or the objection.

DUN DUND

(Yup. She definitely doesn't watch Law & Order.)

So now besides looking like a poofy, orange pumpkin and having my own extremely bad, porcupiney-hair day, Mrs. Pappazian is probably waiting for the moment when she sees me wearing this hat.

Even if technically the hat is called a

fedora.

The thing is . . . Mrs. Pappazian just has no idea what a look at one of my bad-hair days could do to her.

DUN DUND

. . . BREAKING NEWS . . . BREAKING NEWS . . . BREA

six

I give the arms-stretched safety patrol signal to the last first graders, then wave them across the sidewalk. "Always remember, safety first."

Venus is waiting for me at the front door.

"Excellent hat choice, Z. *Molto* retro."

Told Maddie the fedora wasn't weird . . . but V and I agree the coat is another story. I'm swishing so loud I sound like our washing machine.

The coat slows me down, but I do my best to keep up with Venus as we power walk to our lockers.

Running in the hallways is not allowed at HST. That's **Rule #2**. However, none of the teachers realizes that power walking is really slow running. Venus and I always get to our lockers faster than anyone else.

Except today.

The Bashleys are there first.

Molto suspicious, because usually they are in the girls' bathroom combing their hair—which usually doesn't have to be combed anyway.

The Bashleys never have to wear hats.

But as mysterious as The Bashleys not being in the bathroom is, here's the real question: Why are people taking pictures of The Bashleys and their friends in front of our lockers?

Before I can fully investigate, Mrs. Temlock-Fields stops Venus and me by the library door.

Her finger is on her lips.

"Sotto voce."

Italian for "keep quiet." That also goes for noisy coats.

She opens a bakery box.

Cannoli!

Mrs. Temlock-Fields not only likes to speak Italian, she likes to eat Italian too.

Venus: *Grazie*.

Me: *Grazie* ditto.

Mrs. T-F points to the people down the hall.

"A magazine from New York is taking photographs. *Shhhh*."

Besides knowing library stuff, Mrs. Temlock-Fields makes it her business to know all sorts of other business too.

We've never had magazine people at our school before. Last spring a newspaper did an article on Mr. Gasparinetti, the second-grade teacher, because he unicycled to work every day for a whole year.

I thought it was because he didn't want to

pollute and add to global warming, but now I'm wondering if it was just because he used to be in the circus.

(*I'm leaning toward circus. His class uses an awful lot of paper.*)

I take a bite of cannoli. "But why are magazine people in our hallway when it's not even eight o'clock and nobody is supposed to be inside even on a freezing cold day except if you're a fifth-grade safety patrol person like Venus and me?"

"*Sotto voce, bambina!*"

I whisper, "*Scusami*" (*which is Italian for "Excuse me"*). I try not to swish so much either. It's not easy. The hallways at HST have acoustics *bene*.

"Mrs. Pappazian gave them permission weeks ago. The magazine is called *U GrL*. We have it in the periodical section of the Library."

Lightbulb Momento: That's probably why I don't know anything about accessories. I've been reading National Geographics:

```
Capital of Burkina Faso: Ouagadougou
```

Mrs. Temlock-Fields keeps whispering.

(She's one excellent whisperer. I think it's because she's had a lot
of practice, being a librarian.)

"You should have been here five minutes earlier. See that fellow with red hair?"

Venus and I nod as we eat the cannoli.

"He saw Brittany, Ashley, and their friends Olivia and Jaclyn walking down the hall and asked if they would like to be in the photographs."

Venus looks at me. "Cool."

Very.

Having your picture taken for a magazine, even if it's one that you've never heard of before, is extremely *boing* on the coolability meter.

Especially 181 days before sixth grade.

If only I hadn't been slowed down by the poofy coat . . .

Venus wipes cream filling off her sweater.

"Mrs. T-F? Why do they want to take pictures at our school?"

"Oh, I believe Mrs. Pappazian said the magazine

is doing some sort of article about schools named after presidents."

I almost choke on my cannoli.

"Presidents? Presidents of the United States? I can tell them everything they want to know about presidents! I've got a whole book on them in my locker. I'm even doing an extra-credit report on William Howard Taft!"

"That's right, she does," says Venus. "She is. Zoey can even list them in order forward and backward, everyward. I've heard her. Really. Zoey knows all about them. Show her, Zoey. . . ."

"William Howard Taft was three hundred and thirty-two pounds. The teddy bear was named after Theodore Roosevelt. The *S* in Harry S. Truman stands for absolutely nothing."

"*Shhh!* Girls. Yes, yes, yes, Zoey, you know all about the presidents. But knowing about William Howard Taft doesn't have anything to do with the photographs the magazine is taking for this article."

It doesn't? . . .

Well, How much sEnsE does THat make?

How can people not want to know about William Howard Taft? Or Harry? Or Dwight D. and Silent Cal? Very odd, if you ask me *(very, very odd)*.

Mrs. Temlock-Fields thinks giving us another cannoli will keep us quiet. She's wrong.

Cannoli echo too.

Venus and I chew and crunch as we watch a bald guy with not even one speck of fuzz on his head *(true)* walk over and stand next to Ashley. She combs her hair as he holds up a long pole with a broken silver umbrella stuck on top.

Another man with a red ponytail and a tattoo on his arm muscle unravels fat wires that look like black spaghetti. *(Technically, Mrs. T-F would call it bucatini made with squid ink. You don't want to know what squid ink really is. Trust me.)*

Lady in Black is talking to everybody else dressed in black (except for one lady who is wearing camouflage boots). Boot Lady is holding a camera while another camera hangs around her neck. A

88

girl with long, blond, curly hair walks over to a big computer monitor.

I really think that somebody should know that President Truman was number thirty-three, came from Missouri, and liked to play the piano. And why aren't The Bashleys, Olivia, or Jaclyn even holding an official HST Elementary School notebook? *Scusami*, but if you're taking a picture of somebody from a school named after a president, then somebody should be holding a picture of that president. Or someThinG!

Lady in Black moves Ashley and Brittany this way. Then Olivia and Jacyln that way. And I still don't see anything about President Truman.

And then *(because, like I said, the acoustics are so bene)*, I hear Lady in Black say, "Does anyone have something interesting in their locker that we can use in the photographs?" • • •

"I Doo oooooooO

OOOO."

Even I didn't know the hallway could echo like that.

SeveN

Lady in Black turns around.
 Ponytail guy turns around.
 Boot Lady turns around.
 The Bashleys
 & *Friends* of The Bashleys turn around.
 Lady in Black waves at Venus and me.

"Excellent! Come on over and help us. Show me what you've got."

Venus and I power walk over to my locker. There's a lot of swishing, so I try to take off my poofy coat. It gets tangled in my safety patrol belt.

Lady in Black, whose name is Jazz, helps me off with the coat.

"Grabowski's Tool and Die?" she says as I turn around to face my locker.

"It's a bowling shirt," I say as I spin the combination in record time. "My aunt says it's vintage *and* retro."

"Hmm . . . interesting. So . . . Ray, what have you got in that locker of yours?"

"Oh, her name isn't Ray," interrupts Venus. "It's Zoey."

"It's my great-grandfather's shirt; he actually voted for President Truman the year everyone thought he lost. But he really won. It's a totally excellent story. Here—it's all in this book."

I open my locker.

There is a slight

avalanche.

4 books

(My locker is sort of like my room.)

on the presidents of the United States

a thesaurus   pix of **Harrison**   history book

piccolo   crossword puzzles

Louisa May Alcott

LITTLE WOMEN *(Who doesn't want to be Jo?)*

2 owl-puke pellets

a book on

King Tut *(the original celebritini)*

Everything You Always Wanted to Know about Geography BUT Were Afraid to Ask

(Someday Venus and I will visit the Leaning Tower of Pisa and measure how far it really leans.)

3 tennis balls   COLORED Markers

tube of green paint

half-eaten apple   sheet music

and, of course, a roll of orange duct tape

Jazz to Boot Lady: "Fun! Get all of this, Maya."

Click Click Click Click

President Truman?

Click Click

Click **WHT?** Click **Tut?**

Click Click **Big Ben?**

Click Click Click

my **Chucks?** Click owl pellets?

Click fedora?

The Bashleys laugh. Click *Me?*

The *Friends* of The Bashleys laugh.

Click Venus and I look at each other.

Click Click Click

We laugh too! Click

Click.

Jazz snaps her fingers.

Lights switch off.

Ponytail Guy disconnects the bucatini.

Blond lady packs up the computers.

Bald guy collapses the silver umbrella.

"That's a wrap, guys," says Jazz. "Thanks for helping us out with these last couple of shots, Ray. You and the stuff from your locker were a big help. We'll get all the permissions and paperwork from you girls signed later. I'll send proof copies to the school when we get them. Gotta scoot. Remember—Go *U GrL!*"

The Bashleys and *Friends* of The Bashleys shriek and giggle as they head into Mrs. Helferich's room. I try to cram my poofy coat into my locker, and down the hall, Jazz turns and waves.

"That hat's a keeper, Ray!"

The bell rings.

8:00

Arrivederci, Jazz.

eiGht

Venus and I are still stuffing the poofy coat into my locker when suddenly *(that's right)* Mrs. Pappazian swoops in from around the corner.

"Zoey Zinevich! Off with that HAT!"

It's called a fedora.

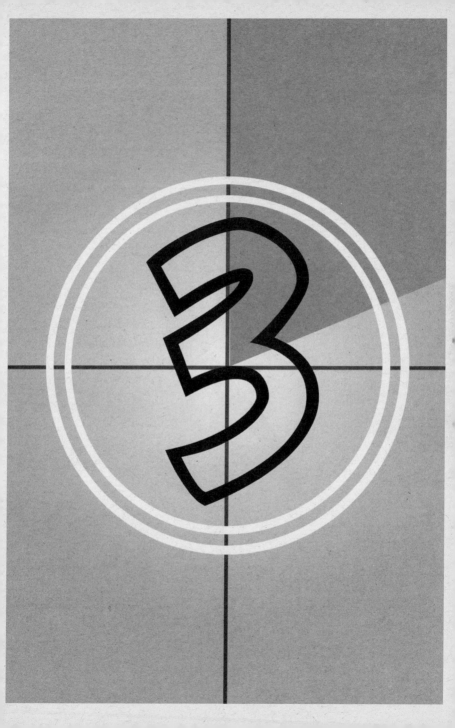

The Lunchroom Life
of
Zoey Zinevich

Part 2

ACT 1: Scene 1 (later that day)

11:37 a.m.

Hot-Lunch Lunch Line

Sent to the principal's office at 11:23, at which time she had to turn in her fedora, Zoey now enters the Lunchroom slash All-Purpose Room slash Gym and is, once again, last in the Harry S. Hot-Lunch Lunch Line.

Mrs. Pappazian was not interested in hearing what Jazz told Zoey.

Not one little bit.

(See previous chapter: "That hat's a keeper, Ray.")

Now, besides all the turkey sandwiches with or without mayo (no tomato) already gone and one incredible bedhead, Zoey also has one incredible hathead. Even Mrs. Salerno, with the mustache that stops

HST Hot-Lunch Lunch Line traffic, is left grumbleless when she sees Zoey and her hair pass by.

The spoon known simply as Super Salerno, filled with a jellied Medley of the Unknown Green Vegetables, misses the plate.

And then . . .

ACT 1: Scene 2

Zoey sees Ashley.
Ashley sees Zoey.
Their eyes meet as they both reach for the last chocolate chip cookie.

ZOEY:
You can have it. I'm really more a chewy oatmeal raisin person.

Ashley doesn't speak.

She only stares, but she does take the cookie.

ACT 1: Scene 3

The two pass the official **LUNCH LIST NAME CHECKER** checkpoint.

The Table Bashley in all its coolness is only steps away. . . .

ZOEY:
Taking those photographs this morning with you and Brittany for the magazine was fun.

ASHLEY:
With you and your geeky sneakers, freaky bowling shirt, owl pellets, frog pictures, weird hat, and Louisa May whoever?
. . . You thought.

You probably ruined all of our
chances to have our pictures in the
magazine. You better not be in any
of our pictures . . . RAY.

Not to be continued.

THE END.

Nine

Table Ten.

"If you want, you can use my hat, Zoey," says Walter Colson.

I take it.

But I can only wear it when the All-Purpose Room is the slash Gym and not the slash Lunchroom. Unfortunately, that's not today.

We don't have phys ed.

114

I know.

This is a short one.

Makes up for number two.
(I'm calling it chapter averaging.)

Z.Z.

115

interr

mezzo

This is sort of a brain break from all the drama.

(I know. It's getting very intense.)

When my grandparents take me to see a play in New York City and it's the end of Act 1, all of a sudden the orchestra goes

TA TA TA TA!

and the curtain comes down, the lights go up, and then everybody goes to the bathroom or gets a candy bar. (Just so you know—you don't have much of a chance of doing either in New York, because the lines are like forever.

But you can do whatever you want here.)

You can also think of this as the seventh-inning stretch—which, incidentally, was started by President Taft, who one time stood up after the top half of the seventh inning during a baseball game to stretch his legs, and everybody else did the same thing.

So . . . stretch.

(It's amazing what you can find out by doing extra credit.)

And now . . .

back to the story.

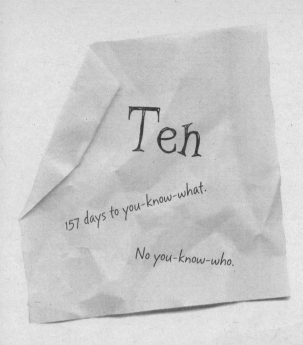

Ten

157 days to you-know-what.

No you-know-who.

I know. You're probably asking,
   "What happened to all
      of those days in between?"

Nothing.

Do you know how sometimes when you're reading a book, you come to the middle or after the middle, and you say to yourself, "Huh?" or "Boring," or "Snooze. Nothing is happening"?

This is one of those parts.

But if you really want to read boring stuff, well, okay. Here it is.

CAUTION: The following may cause drowsiness. Read at your own risk. Permission to skip ahead.

1. I tried hair gel.

    It was a fiasco.

       fi • as • co

      pronunciation: fE-as-kO

      : a complete failure

2. Luckily, Mrs. Pappazian returned the fedora.

3. Alex Shemtob said he loved me . . .

    when my hair was gelled!

    (I know—I know—I know.)

He told me in science class as we were dissecting an owl pellet. Our yellow plastic tweezers, technically called forceps, touched as we discovered a mouse tibia at the same time.

Then he gave me a green HB pencil.

My stomach felt all icky and my face got hot. I didn't know if it was because of the owl pellet, discovering a mouse bone, or Alex.

My mother said when I get older (and I'm pretty sure she means older than eleven), I will remember it as romantic and sweet. (Yes, she really said that.)

TMI.

I don't want to think about that right now when I'm only ten and seven-eighths.

But HBs are the best, so . . . I'm keeping the pencil.

4. A very strange thing is happening to my body.

My earlobes are growing.

Do you know what my mother said?

. . . Here's what my mother said:

"What an imagination you have, Zoey."

. . . Oh really?

My Auntie Barbara has earlobes that are so long, they swing back and forth. On her, earrings are dangerous weapons. A mosquito buzzing around her head is a goner.

5. Jazz sent the school the photographs that are in the magazine. There are pictures of The Bashleys and the Friends of The Bashleys. (They are sort of out of focus, and the hallway and lockers are more in focus.) There are also pictures of Harry, WHT, Big Ben, Harrison, and my bowling shirt (back and front pocket), fedora feather, one sneaker, and a close-up of my braces.

The Bashleys think that is funny in the extreme. And . . . not cool or chic (noun or adjective).

6. No sign of a fairy godmother. My idea of having one of those has been a fiasco (see number one).

(Told you. Snoozerama. Don't have time for the toe story. Maybe later.)

Eleven

Beeeeeeee-eeeee-eeeeeep.

ATTENTION, PLEASE.
. . . Zoey Zinevich,
report to the
principal's office.

Me? That Zoey Zinevich?

To the principal's office?

Sixteen pairs of eyeballs—not counting the ones belonging to Mrs. Helferich—are eyeballing the person in desk five, row three.

Me.

This is all curiouser and more curiouser, because I have never been called to the principal's office on the loudspeaker. . . .

Not even when I had to turn in the fedora.

(That was only a Hall Call.)

Mrs. Helferich is stunned by this surprising, ugly turn of events too. She hands me the hall pass, because if you don't have a hall pass and you're caught in the hall without having a hall pass, you're going to have big trouble.

You have broken `Rule #8`:

`You MUST Have a Hall Pass.`

Since I'm already called over the loudspeaker, I don't need any more trouble. I hold on to the hall pass and power walk to Mrs. Pappazian's office. Does a hall pass work like a . . .

Get-out-of-Jail-Free Card?

Or does it mean . . .
Go Directly to the Office.
Do Not Pass Go.
Do Not Go to the Bathroom.

Is a fifth grader allowed in a second-grade girls' bathroom . . . ?

Mrs. Katterman, the school secretary, is on the phone as I walk into the Main Office.

She waves me in behind the **COUNTER**.

Uh-oh. Nobody ever goes behind the **COUNTER** in the Main Office unless Mrs. Katterman waves you in. Or you have a broken nose. Mika Sanderberg got a broken nose when a volleyball hit her in the face during gym period.

The nurse wasn't in school that day, so Mrs. Shulman, the gym teacher who is lucky because she gets to wear sweatpants every day, took Mika to the principal's office. Mrs. Katterman waved her in behind the **COUNTER** immediately!

Mika told Venus and me all about it. Her nasal septum got smashed. *(Technically, that means the membrane thingie dividing her nostrils wasn't ever going to be dividing anything again, unless she had an operation, which she did.)*

Mika dripped blood on the **COUNTER** and also behind the **COUNTER**.

Having a broken nose and dripping real blood is the only reason I've ever heard of somebody getting waved behind Mrs. Katterman's **COUNTER**.

Unless you are in really **BIG** trouble.

Mrs. Katterman is still on the phone.

"Well, yes, I will do that. . . ."

I've never noticed it before . . . but Mrs.

Katterman has very big earlobes.

"Yes. Absolutely. I understand. I will get back to you shortly."

I smile.

Mrs. Katterman doesn't smile back.

She hangs up the phone.

She stares.

I clear my throat. Swallow. Whisper.

"I'm Zoey Zinevich."

"WHO? Speak up. Don't garble. All you kids garble. Speak clearly when you're spoken to."

"I'm Zoey Zinevich."

"Don't raise your voice, young lady. Didn't I call your name over the loudspeaker?"

I nod.

Not too big. Not too little. Just right.

Mrs. Katterman nods back. An okay-you-nodded-back-correctly nod.

She opens her desk drawer.

She closes her desk drawer.

She puts a pencil in her pencil holder.

She sighs.

She gets up from behind her desk, very s l o w l y.

Then she walks over to Mrs. Pappazian's closed door even s l o w e r.

Mrs. Katterman knocks. She opens the door a little and peeks in.

Only her head does the peeking. The rest of Mrs. Katterman can't fit.

"Do you want to see Zoey Zinevich now?"

I hear Mrs. Pappazian from the other side of the door: "Send her in."

I power walk toward the door.

Suddenly, Mrs. Katterman stops me.

"You don't have gum in your mouth, do you? You know we don't allow gum chewing."

HST RULE #6:
Absolutely No Chewing Gum!

"I know. I don't chew gum. I haven't chewed gum for one year, two months, and twenty-four days . . . braces."

"You kids always say that, but I know you pouch. I know you swallow, with or without those braces. Those braces are just an excuse. We know you chew. You can't fool us."

"I'm not fooling."

I open my mouth.

Mrs. Katterman squeezes her eyes to itsy slits.

"Okay . . . well . . . go in."

I walk into Mrs. Pappazian's office.

It smells like . . . someone eating Chinese food at her desk? Are those duck sauce stains I see on one of those folders?

Mrs. Pappazian.

In Her Office.

With the Chinese Noodles.

She shuffles a stack of folders on her desk and smiles without looking at me.

"The reason I called you down to the office is because . . ."

I'm pretty much wondering that myself because—

    a. I'm not chewing gum.
    b. I'm not wearing my fedora.
    c. I'm not dripping blood.
    d. I have a hall pass.

And most important, how much trouble can I be in when Mrs. Pappazian hasn't fallen face-first onto her duck sauce–stained folders after seeing me hatless?

I squeeze my eyes into itsy slits just like Mrs. Katterman and stare at Mrs. Pappazian. Then I stop because it's really giving me a headache.

Sitting in the principal's office is all curiouser and curiouser. Especially when everything smells like pork lo mein.

". . . Miss Jazz Duval, the creative director of the magazine that was here several weeks ago taking photographs, called today to leave a message for . . . you."

". . . *Me?*"

"She would like to speak with you and your parents."

". . . *Me?*"

"She asked that you call her."

". . . *Me?*"

". . . Yes. *You* . . . Zoey Zinevich."

B-r-rr-rrrrr-rrrrr-inG

Stay tuned for an episode of

Phone Chat with Zoey Zinevich

with

Mother
Father
Brother
Aunt Rootie

. . . and Four-Year-Old Sister

Maddie: "I'll get it!"

    Mom: "I'll get it!"

        Stewart: "I'll get it!"

           Aunt Rootie: "I'll get it!"

              Me: "I'll get it!"

Dad: "No. I'll get it."

"Hello? Miss Duval?

Yes. Yes, it is.

Well, of course. Uh-huh. Agree.

Yes. Uh-huh . . . Yes. Yes.

Of course . . .

              Mrs. Zinevich?

Right here . . ."

"Hello? Miss Duval?

Yes. Yes, it is.

Well, of course. Uh-huh. Agree.

Yes. Uh-huh . . . Yes. Yes.

Of course . . .

              Aunt Rootie?

              Aunt Rootie.

Yes. Right here . . ."

"Hello? Miss Duval?
Yes. Yes, it is.
Well, of course. Uh-huh. Agree.
Yes. Uh-huh . . . Yes. Yes.
Of course . . .
                    Mr. Zinevich?
Right here . . ."

"Hello? Miss Duval?
Yes. Yes, it is.
Well, of course. Uh-huh. Agree.
Yes. Uh-huh . . . Yes. Yes.
Of course . . .
Zoey?
She's right here . . ."

"Hello? Jazz? . . .
Yes. It's me, Zoey."

Twelve

Really quick update:

So, this is what I'm thinking. • • •
I really can't do much thinking. Or dot connecting.
I have to go to bed *muy pronto*.
(Venus told me that's Spanish for "very quick.")

Tomorrow morning I am going to NYC (New York City) to meet with Jazz and her magazine people. (I didn't even know she had "people.") Actually, she's picking me up in a limousine, which I know isn't environmentally correct, but Jazz said it was a

140

hybrid, so my carbon footprint will still be neutral.

So I'm not thinking so I can go to sleep.

Except, I can't stop thinking . . .

so I keep thinking.

I don't really know how this all happened.
I only know that it happened, and when it happened, it was all *Molto excitinG!*

Jazz's note said she would call at 6:00.

From her office.

And exactly at 6:00 she actually called,
and it was all *Molto excitinG!*

She asked me to come to her office and

meet her people because they want to
do an article on ME, which—I know!—is

Molto Molto excitinG!

(Did she really say "article"?)

Well, I can't remember exactly
what she said, or what she called it,

only that she said

somethinG, and it was all

Molto excitinG!

141

Venus and Aunt Rootie are coming with me too (because my parents won't let me go alone, blah blah blah), but they also think it's all *Molto Molto!*

And luckily we have a day off from school for something or other—so we aren't even breaking any **Harry S. Truman Rules.**

Jazz said for me to wear my bowling shirt, great-grandpop's fedora, my Chucks, and not to even comb my hair • • •

which, actually • • •

when I keep thinking about it, doesn't sound very exciting.

In fact, it sounds sort of weird.

But, Venus says, her sister says it's because Jazz is probably going to give me a complete, total, and unbelievably cool

Molto **chic** makeover—which is

Molto exciting!

Which makes me think, even though I shouldn't be thinking because I should be sleeping, that maybe . . . just maybe . . . a fairy godmother somewhere out wherever FGs hang out connected my dots.

Molto excitinG!

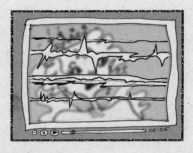

"Here I am! FG #11-288! Good to go with an incredible, cool make-over for one Zoey Zinevich."

"R-r-r-r-ead-d-d R-r-r-r-d-d R-r-r-ead-d-d-dd-dd-d-d-d-d"

"Ready, Zoey?"

"Jazz?. . . Jazz!"
I should have guessed.
Lightbulb Momento: She's way 21st
century.

146

Hair?

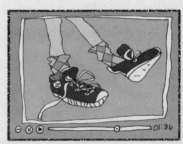

Feet?

"Get ready for one La-di-da
Incredible, Chic Makeover!"

"Cool."

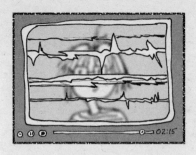

"J-j-j-j-aa J-ja-aa-zzz-z-zz?"

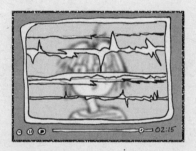

"J-j-j-j-aa J-ja-aa-zzz-z-zz?"

Tune in tomorrow.
*(That's called a cliff-hanger.
It's very dramatic.)*

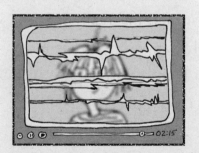

"J-j-j-j-aa J-ja-aa-zzz-z-zz?"

149

Thirteen

TA-TA-TA-TA!

I knew it was all very logical. Connect that dot to this dot to that dot, just like Mrs. Helferich always says.

When you wish for something really hard, it can really, most definitely happen: There is most definitely a limousine in front of my house, 156 days to sixth grade. Ha! Cool Police!

Jazz gets out of the car, and there's lots of introductions with my parents, blah blah blah, blah blah blah; then good-byes, etc. etc. etc.; and finally Aunt Rootie, Venus, Jazz, and I get into the car.

It's a hybrid Hummer, so I think I'm still EC.

Our driver, Howard, closes the door. He's sort of like a Cinderella chauffeur but in a regular suit and tie, with a gray mustache that is very bushy. We all buckle up and are good to go.

"We have juices, breakfast tacos with guacamole, strawberries, and . . ." Jazz holds out a box. "Donuts."

Howard starts the car *(I mean Hummer)*.

Venus looks at me and grins. It's a very *chic* breakfast. We take one of everything.

The heated seat *(or maybe it's the taco)* gets to Aunt Rootie, and she falls asleep before we get to the turnpike. Luckily she doesn't snore, and she's wearing her big sunglasses so none of us can see her eyes flutter. Which they always do when she sleeps.

Aunt Rootie misses seeing the Statue of Liberty. *(It's sort of far away, but Venus has binoculars.)* She wakes up just as the car goes through the toll plaza and heads into the tunnel. It's really quite unbelievable. We are underwater even though it doesn't feel like we're underwater.

Walter Colson should definitely do an extra-credit report on it. It is a totally major engineering phenomenon.

(Walter is very good at building things. Last year he built a model of the Roman Coliseum out of sugar cubes.)

We drive out of the tube, which is another name for the tunnel, and Howard makes a left turn at the traffic light. Aunt Rootie, who is now very awake, starts shouting.

"Howard. Howard! Turn right at this next light! You beat the traffic that way. I've been driving in this city for years. Trust me."

Howard nods, but I don't think he needs help from Aunt Rootie. He drives right between a bus and three taxis. *Molto* amazing. Venus and I look out the windows and count how many people Howard almost runs over before we get to Jazz's office.

Howard zigs, zags, and then makes a right turn. Our people count is eighteen and a half.

Jazz reaches into her bag and pulls out her

phone. She flips it open. Howard turns the car closer to the curb.

"Hey, Hoyt. JD. We're pulling up. Tell everyone to get ready." *("JD." Jazz is so you-know-what.)*

"Ready for what?" I ask.

Jazz smiles. "You'll see."

Venus leans closer to me and whispers,

"The incredible, cool makeover."

I nod and smile as Howard gets out of the car and walks around to the sidewalk, where he opens the door.

"Okay. Everybody out," says Jazz. "Thank you, Howard." She glances at her watch. "We'll see you again in about a little over an hour."

(An hour? Magazine people can do an incredible, cool makeover in only an hour? They are almost as fast as a real fairy godmother.)

"Follow me, everyone," Jazz says as she turns to go into the building.

I look up. This building is really, really, **seriously** really tall.

"Did I ever tell you girls about the time I was

153

almost a Rockette?" says Aunt Rootie, as she follows us through the revolving doors into the lobby.

"You were almost a Rockette?" we all say. Our voices echo. This lobby has acoustics way more *bene* than even the hallway at HST.

Aunt Rootie laughs as Jazz gathers the three of us by the long security counter.

(It's something like the one Mrs. Katterman has in the office, only this one is marble and Mrs. Katterman's is plastic. The security guard looks like he's even harder to get past than Mrs. Katterman.)

"They're with me," Jazz says, showing him her identification badge. "Come with me, ladies."

We snake through the red velvet ropes and head for a long double row of elevators.

One of the doors in the middle right row opens and we step inside. Jazz pushes a button that lights up with the number forty-two.

My ears pop.

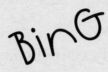

The door opens. "Welcome to *U GrL!*"

We step into the reception area and face the name of the magazine in big orange and purple letters on the back wall.

SMaRt!

U GrL!

UniqUE!

CleveR!

The walls are painted the same color as my wicked green stickies.

Venus whispers, "Very cool."

A girl gets up from behind a desk and takes our coats. *(Luckily my mother didn't make me wear my poofy coat.)*

Jazz crooks her finger for us to follow. We go down a hall with lots of offices and turn left. Then right. Then left. Right. Left.

We finally reach a door at the end of a long hall that says **Conference Room**.

Jazz smiles at me. "Ready?"

"Ready!" *(Coolability meter, get ready to boing.)*

Jazz opens the door.

Aunt Rootie gasps.

Venus gasps.

I think I have to go to the bathroom.

If this is my makeover, it's going to be very weird. Everyone is wearing fedoras, sneakers, and bowling shirts with names embroidered on their pockets.

. . . They all look like me!

(Especially the one who looks like she hasn't combed her hair.)

fourteen

Jazz puts her arm around me.

"This is our Zoey!"

Everyone applauds.

(Applause? Getting weirder.)

"Hello, Zoey. I'm Cindy Fowler, the executive editor of *U GrL*. So nice to meet you."

The lady with short, white hair shakes my hand. "We are so excited to have you here."

"You are?"

Jazz laughs. "Can't you tell?"

I look at everyone wearing fedoras that look just like mine *(or technically my great-grandpop's).*

Well, actually ● ● ● no.

The Executive Editor Person picks up a magazine from the conference table and opens the pages to where the green sticky notes are stuck.

"Zoey, I'm sure by now you've seen all the photographs of you in the issue of *U Grl.*"

"You mean, my hat . . . and bowling shirt . . . and . . ."

"sneakers!"

A girl named China comes forward and twirls in purple Chucks.

That taco isn't feeling too good right about now. The orange juice is doing slosh-dancing in my digestive tract too.

The Following Is a Public Service Factoid:

Complete digestion actually takes a while to occur in the human body. After swallowing, food goes down the esophagus in approximately five seconds, but it hangs around in your stomach for a couple of hours. Then travels on.

(No need for further explanation)

"Zoey, when we put our last issue together, we never thought we would get the kind of response that we did—but we did."

I look at Jazz and hear my stomach grumble. "You didn't? I mean, you did?"

"We did. And most of the responses were about you."

Grumble. "Me?"

"In fact, we received so many emails, it crashed our server."

Venus sucks in more air. "It did?"

"It did," says Jazz. "We had questions about the hat, bowling shirt, frogs, crossword puzzles— we must have gotten hundreds of questions from girls wanting to know about Louisa May Alcott."

"Well, she is a very good writer."

"Yes, we know," says EEP. "And now a whole lot of other girls, who perhaps didn't know before, know that too."

Jazz points. "Do you see that huge pile of letters at the end of the table?"

I nod and stomach-grumble. Stomach-grumble and nod.

"Well, those are only a sampling of the ones we received from girls all over the country. Go on, Zoey. Read a couple."

I do.

She's right.

They did.

This is now:

OFFICIALLY WEIRD.

"I'm not sure I understand any of this."

The Executive Editor Person with short, white hair laughs. *(Weirder, because none of this is funny.)*

"Zoey, *U GrL* celebrates girls who are unique. Girls who are thoughtful. Curious. Girls who are inventive. Smart. Girls who *do*. Girls who *think*. And girls who have their own style and flair while doing it. Since the last issue came out, our readers have been telling us—that's you."

Backspace. Did she say . . . *me*?

I look at Venus and Aunt Rootie. They look like they could make a bathroom trip too.

"But-but-but-but . . . uh . . ."

"Yes, Zoey?"

"Well . . . the thing is . . . I mean . . . you know . . . do you know? . . . I'm only not even eleven. And I don't even know anything about accessorization either. Unless you count duct tape. Oh, yes, sure, maybe I'm good at making woven backpacks, but that's it. Okay, one wallet too. But that's it! And let me tell you, I don't look good in pink. At all. I'm a green person."

I take off the fedora. "Look, look! I don't know how to use a round brush except to paint watercolors, and Venus is way better at that than I am. I tried gel, and it was a fiasco-disasco. Ask Venus. She'll tell you."

Venus nods. "It wasn't good."

Jazz laughs. "But Zoey, you do know lots of other things. And that's what's interesting to us at *U GrL*. And to our readers. They're interested in all sorts of different things."

"Even the presidents of the United States?"

"Well, I don't know if anyone is as interested in that particular subject as you are, but that's fine."

"It is?"

Jazz motions to a person with a bowling shirt that has "Bebe" embroidered on the pocket. She fans out big boards on the table.

"Here are some layout ideas for the spreads we want to feature in upcoming issues. Hoyt—you remember my assistant, don't you?" Hoyt waves. "He remembered the books in your locker; and we had all the photos that Maya took during the photo shoot, so we got our inspiration from them."

Jazz picks up one of the boards that has pictures of me all over it.

"We were thinking of taking a photo or two in front of President Theodore Roosevelt's house."

"He was the only president to be born in New York City," I blurt. *(Can't help it. I'm a natural blurter.)*

162

"I'm pretty sure the house is on Twentieth Street."

All the magazine people laugh.

(I really am missing the humor here.)

"You're right," says Jazz.

Hoyt points back to the boards. "And we're planning locations in places like perhaps the Guggenheim, the Met, the planetarium, the American Museum of Natural History . . . the Staten Island Ferry. . . ."

I look at Jazz. "I think I still don't get it."

"Zoey, we believe you are the perfect person to write a diary or column for the magazine representing our readers with your thoughts. Things you like to do. Places you visit."

"Maybe even do a blog," says EEP. "A blog on our website would be very cool indeed."

Indeed? *("Indeed" is like one of my most dollar-word choices.)*

Are my ears buzzing now too or is that Hoyt's phone?

"How does all of this sound, Zoey?"

"Writing for your magazine? *Me?* Sounds yes,

you know . . . indeed . . . what you said. But are you really sure you want *me*? Because, really Jazz . . . I'mnotthatcoolI'mnotevenalittlecoolI'm souncoolIneedafairygodmothertomakemecoolbe foresixthgradereallytrulymyarrowiswaydownon TheBashleycoolabilitymeterVenusandIneversitat TheTableBashley.Wesitat . . . Table Ten."

Jazz looks at me, then at Venus.

"The who? The what? When? Where?"

I take a deep breath.

"Everybody at my school thinks Zoey Zinevich is . . . well . . . a sort of . . .

geek."

"Geek chic!" shouts Aunt Rootie.

Did she really just say that? *Geek Chic?* My own aunt is *so* not helping this situation.

"Geek chic? LOVE IT!" cries EEP, while Jazz's people rush to find a pencil to write it down.

Can this get any worse?

Geek chic?

Something has gotten all mixed up here.

This is not the happening I exactly wanted to happen.

Jazz smiles. "So, Zoey? Ready to be *U GrL's* very own . . . *'geekanista'*?"

Okay—

(. . . Wait-Wait-Wait!

Lightbulb Momento!

I know what this is.

This is one of those weird "other dimension" things

that Simon Malachek always talks about.

It's when everything gets all weird and backward and sideways,

and nothing makes any sense. But then

you wake up or pinch yourself or whatever,

and everything is the way it's supposed to be.

Yes. Uh-huh. Absolutely.

A weird other dimension.

That's what this is.)

EY

ONE

Ouch!

Or not.

It's still Fedora and Bowling Shirt Central.

Stomach is still grumbling.

Probably have a black-and-blue mark.

And Jazz is not a fairy godmother.

"Jazz? Can I ask you one question?"

"Of course."

"Does this mean you're not really going to give me an incredible, cool makeover? Ever?"

Jazz puts her arm around me.

"A makeover? Now why would Zoey Zinevich ever want one of those?"

fifteen

Three days later . . .

So this is what I'm thinking • • •
being almost eleven is still very complicated.
Especially when you don't have a fairy godmother.

But sometimes . . .
stuff isn't so hard to figure out on your own
after all.

All-New Episodes of

The Lunchroom Life
of
Zoey Zinevich

ACT 1: Scene 1

11:28 a.m.

The Hot-Lunch Lunch Line

Venus and Zoey are once again last in the Hot-Lunch Lunch Line. They have stayed after library class to help Mrs. Temlock-Fields in the Media Center. She is still teaching them Italian. Today they learn "*magnifico*," which means "magnificent," "superb," and "fantastic." Zoey and Venus also decide to translate it as "most excellent."

The girls inch along the Hot-Lunch Lunch Line after passing the slumgullion plop of the Super Salerno and the **OFFICIAL CHECK** of Mrs. Petrovic, and then they find themselves standing behind . . .

The Bashleys.

ASHLEY AND BRITTANY:
Venus! Zoey! Zoey! Venus!

ASHLEY:
Is it true what we've been hearing?

BRITTANY:
Yes, is it really true? Everyone has been talking, even Mrs. Temlock-Fields, and she only usually just whispers.

ASHLEY:
Zoey, are you really really going to have your own column—and blog—

BRITTANY:
—in *U GrL* magazine? Like having your picture in it, and everything and so on and so on and so on?

ZOEY:

Maybe. I guess. They asked me. Not sure. But, probably. . . uh, yes.

BRITTANY:

Very VERY cool! Very very.

VENUS:

It's *magnifico*, is what it is.

ASHLEY:

Absolutely! *Magni* . . . what Venus just said. *Magni* . . . you know.

BRITTANY:

We want to know everything about the whole day from both of you.

ASHLEY:

EVERYTHING as in ALL. You have to tell us what you did. What you said.

BRITTANY:

So come sit with us!

ASHLEY:

Yes, sit at our table!

An incredible happening has just
incredibly happened. Zoey and Venus
have just been asked by **The Bashleys**
to sit at **The Table Bashley**. *And only the*
you-know-who
Venus looks at Zoey. *get to sit there.*

Zoey looks at Venus.

Zoey sees Alex Shemtob inhaling
and Walter Colson polka-dotting. It's
an easy multiple-choice. . . . Zoey
smiles and turns to **The Bashleys**.

ZOEY:

Thanks for asking, Ashley. You
too, Brittany. But, actually, Venus
and I sit at . . .

Table

Ten.

ZOEY:

If you want . . . you can join us.

Venus and Zoey and their trays filled with plates of slumgullion and a jellied Medley of the Unknown Green Vegetables walk past **The Table Bashley** to **Table Ten**.

They sit between Simon Malachek and Walter Colson's spiky hair, and right across from Alex Shemtob.

The girls are not wearing their art smocks.

They do not care.

The End

Just so you know,
this is not like the last
chapter of my whole
entire life.
After all, I am only
almost eleven.

(But I'm thinking—
it's pretty magnifico.)
Z.Z

Oh—remember that Toe Story
I was supposed to tell you?

It really isn't that important.

Chic ZoCabulary

arrivederci: Italian for "till we meet again," "good-bye" pronunciation: ar-E-vA-der-chE syn: *adios, au revoir, sayonara*

avalanche: n. a mass of stuff waiting to happen in my locker

backstory: n. fill in the blank spill; info that you don't know, but should know

b-friend: n. best friend

Bashleys, The: n. combination name for Brittany & Ashley (as in, Zoey + Venus = Zenus)

bene: n. or adj. Italian for *magnifico*, (*bella, buono*) good

boing: adj. wow on the coolability meter < duct tape is boing >

bucatini: n. fat spaghetti

cannoli: n. an Italian crispy pastry filled with creamy stuff < Mrs. Temlock-Fields's favorite dessert > pronunciation: Ka-nO-Lee

carbon footprint: n. a measure of the effect human activity has on the environment, calculated in units of carbon dioxide; your 'personal planet polluting profile' (aka E-4P)

celebritini: n. Venus-Zoey speak for famous person

coolability: n. extreme cool < the coolability meter went boing >

curiouser: adj. odd; strange Google: Alice in W-land

dewey decimal: n. duh. (Have you never used the library!)

digital: v. to take a brain picture (see Chapter Three)

disasco: n. see *fiasco*

dollar word choice: adj. see *primo*

EC: adj. environmentally correct < do the right thing and be EC >

factoid: n. bite of info

fairy dust intervention: n. Big Time Help from a Fairygodmother

fedora: n. spiffy hat

fiasco: n. a disaster < using hair gel can result in a fiasco-disasco >

global warming: n. earth fever < as the Captain of the *Titanic* should have said, "Pay attention to those icebergs!" >

hybrid hummer: n. according to Venus, an "eco-cool set of wheels"

intermezzo: n. Italian for a "short break"

lactose intolerant: n. or adj. inability to digest milk products (You really don't want me to use this in a sentence.)

larvae: n. plural of larva worm-like stage of insect life process (icky, yet interesting)

Lightbulb Momento: n. aha!

M-W: n. *Merriam-Webster*

magnifico: adj. Italian for "even better *bene*," "most excellent ever"

massive: adj. huge, big

mathlete: n. a person who is most excellent in mathematics

Millard: n. (1) my stuffed bunny; (2) first name of the thirteenth president, who was a Whig, but didn't wear one

molto: adj. Italian for "very" < bullfrog catching is *molto* exciting >

owl pellets: n. the end products of an owl's digestive process

peruse: v. read with interest < I peruse my dictionary >

power walk: v. slow running

primo: adj. the best

retro: n. or adj. old school new cool

Samuel Morse-ing: adj. getting help; from the inventor, Samuel Morse (Google-worthy)

serious double digits n. old (like maybe thirteen or something)

slumgullion: n. still a mystery

snickerfest: n. big ha-ha

snoozerama: n. BORING

unequivocally: adv. for sure!

vintage: n. or adj. retro chic with a side dish of extra coolness

wedgie: adj. stuck BIG TIME

wicked: adj. cool; fierce; "the ultima-ta-ta" < as in: wicked green stickies >

geek chic:
gEk shEk

unique, unusual, individual style and flair
(hair not included)

Margie Palatini is the author of more than two dozen outrageously funny and award-winning books for children, including MOO WHO?, illustrated by Keith Graves; THE PERFECT PET, illustrated by Bruce Whatley; the Bad Boys series, illustrated by Henry Cole; THE CHEESE, illustrated by Steve Johnson and Lou Fancher; and NO BITING, LOUISE, illustrated by Matthew Reinhart. You can visit her online at www.margiepalatini.com.

Visit Zoey online at
www.geekchicthezoeyzone.com.